D1110057

"When people mess with me about my longboard, I get nervous. I feel like I can't just be myself, and that messes with how I ride. Ugh! Why can't I just get over it?!"

LEI TÍAN
Age: 14
Hometown: Just a place in California

STONE ARCH BOOKS

presents

TONY HAWK

LIVE 2 SKATE

DARING

written by

BLAKE A. HOENA

images by

NDO CANO AND LAURA RIVERA

a

CAPSTONE

production

Published by Stone Arch Books
A Capstone Imprint
1710 Roe Crest Drive, North Mankato, Minnesota 56003
www.capstonepub.com

Printed in Canada.
042014   008086FRF14

Library of Congress Cataloging-in-Publication Data is
available on the Library of Congress website.
Hardcover: 978-1-4342-9139-4
Paperback: 978-1-4342-9142-4
eBook: 978-1-4965-0086-1

Summary: Lei and her crew feel threatened when a group of
older kids try to claim the skatepark as their own.

Designer: Bob Lentz
Creative Director: Heather Kindseth

Design Elements: Shutterstock

CHAPTERS

For Lei Tian, the day started off like any normal Saturday. Her brother's pug nosed his way into her bedroom as she slept and then started gnawing on her red Cons. Feng had named his dog "Chewy." Not because he was a huge *Star Wars* geek — though he was — but because that's what his dog did. Chewed on everything: sticks, towels, toys, chair legs. Even Lei's shoes.

Lei's sleepy brain was slow to process the noises Chewy made as he happily chomped on one shoe. When she finally realized what was happening, she tossed aside her blankets and scrambled to the foot of her bed.

There was Chewy, tugging on her laces.

"Stop that!" she yelled.

Leaning over the edge of her bed, Lei rescued the shoe, yanking it away. Chewy growled and playfully shook his head, as if he were hoping for a game of tug-of-war. But Lei wasn't up for messing around with her red Cons. They were her favorite skate shoes. Luckily, Chewy was an old dog — all gums and few teeth. He slobbered more than he chewed. Still, that had its drawbacks.

"Ew, gross," Lei said as she held up the shoe by the toe. A string of drool hung from the laces.

"*Grrr-arf! Gr-arf!*" Chewy barked. Then he attacked her other shoe.

"Hey, knock that off," Lei yelled.

She quickly nudged Chewy out the door.

Lei sat in bed, arms crossed. She was fuming. Not only had she been woken up early, but her skate shoes were covered in dog slobber. She bet Feng let Chewy into her room on purpose. She really wished he'd stop messing with her.

I suppose that's just what older brothers do, she thought. *Make life difficult for their little sisters.*

Once she cooled off, Lei got up and quickly dressed, pulling a Spitfire T-shirt over her head and slipping on a pair of ripped jeans. Tying up her Cons was a struggle since the laces were still a bit slimy. Then she burst through her bedroom door, nearly stepping on Chewy. He went for her shoelaces.

"No, you don't!" she said, wagging a finger at the dog.

"*Grrr-arf! Gr-arf!*" he barked back at her, wanting to play.

"Don't excite him," her grandmother called from the kitchen. "Come eat your breakfast."

Lei walked into the kitchen and plopped down next to her grandfather. He had his face buried in the morning newspaper and grunted, "Good morning, little one," as she stole a slice of toast from his plate. Her grandmother then set a bowl of gooey white rice in front of her. There was an over-easy egg dropped in the middle of the gruel, and bacon chunks were scattered about.

"Aw, congee again," Lei whined. "I need some Sugar Os to give me a boost. I'm hitting the skatepark with my crew."

"Protein's better than sugar," was all her grandmother said as she filled up a glass of OJ for Lei.

Breakfast congee was her grandmother's way of trying to make a traditional, yet American breakfast. Lei wasn't so sure that she was hitting the mark, though. Something about white rice, white toast, and white egg just didn't seem all that American to her. Lei poked the egg with her toast to let the runny yellow yoke mix with the whiteness of the congee.

Good thing I've got some trail mix in my pack, she thought.

Lei used the toast to dab at the egg yolk and scoop up pieces of bacon. As she ate, she mixed up the congee to make it look like she had eaten some of it. Then she patted her grandfather on the shoulder and excused herself from the table.

"Don't fall off that thing and hurt yourself," he grumbled.

"Yes, Grandpapa," she replied.

Next to the front door was her Sector 9 longboard, a hand-me-down from her brother. The grip tape had been scuffed up and nearly worn down to the wood in places, but it was still her favorite deck. Actually, it was the only board she could afford. But she had added some ABEC 7 bearings and Butterball wheels. Her longboard could roll for blocks with just one push, and it bombed down hills.

On her way out, Lei also grabbed her backpack. It was filled with her gear and pads. As the door slammed shut behind her, she set her board down on the sidewalk. Pushing forward, Lei heard Chewy barking after her. He was up on the back of the couch and watching her from the front window.

Feng used to take Chewy for rides on this very deck, she thought. *Maybe he misses cruisin' around.*

As she rolled down the sidewalk, Lei popped her earbuds in and plugged into her cell phone. She hit her Cruisin' playlist, and songs started thumping into her ears.

The sidewalks in her neighborhood were cracked and tilted every which way. Her wheels made a loud *ka-tunk, ka-tunk* as she rolled over the broken pavement. And even though she had 75mm wheels and could roll over almost anything, the ride was rough. Whenever traffic cleared, she carved down the side of the street instead.

A few blocks from her house, she jumped on a paved bike trail. She could fly on the smooth pavement.

The trail wound behind some houses and through a wooded park. At night, she wouldn't dare take this route. She'd heard stories about people getting held up and robbed in the dark. But during the day, she didn't worry. Hardly anyone used the trail.

Without an audience, Lei felt daring. Like she could just be herself and try out some moves — things she wouldn't be able to do once she hit the skatepark. Her friends were only interested in street tricks, grinding and ollieing. That was fine with her. But there was an art to longboarding that went beyond just getting from point A to point B. Her friends didn't get that.

She switched her playlist to Dancin', and rhythmic beats started throbbing in her ears. Her friends would razz her if they knew what she was groovin' to, but she liked the catchy rhythms. She started cross stepping to the dance beat, stepping up and down her board as she carved down the bike trail.

As she danced on her board, Lei lost herself in the beat of the music. The swaying of her board carving back and forth lulled her into feeling secure and confident. She decided to throw some tricks into her routine. At one point, she stepped toward the front of her board and did a shuvit by leaning on its nose and pushing the back of the board

with her back foot so that the tail spun around out in front. Another time, as she was near the back, she popped up the board by stepping on the tail. She caught its nose in her hand. Then she spun the board around in a 360, hopping back on as it hit the pavement. She had never tried it before, so she was surprised to land it on her first attempt.

SKATEPARK

About a mile down the trail, the run-down houses gave way to a park. On one end was a basketball court, with nets missing from the metal rims of the basketball hoops. On the other end were the remains of an old skatepark. That's where Lei's friends were hanging out.

Marie sat on the pyramid in the middle of the park while three boys huddled around her. Javon and Mike were kind of facing Lei's direction, each of them gripping their boards by the nose. Raul was standing with his back to her, one foot on his deck as he toed it back and forth on the pavement.

They must have been having an intense conversation. No

one noticed as she cut through a break in the chain-link fence that surrounded the skatepark.

She kicked her board forward to build up speed. Just then Javon looked in her direction. She placed a finger to her lips. He said nothing.

As she neared her friends, she shifted her weight to her front foot and swung the tail of her board around for a powerslide. With her wheels screeching across the pavement, her friends all bailed, except for Raul. He stood his ground.

Lei's trick didn't turn out as she had planned. With Raul smiling his crooked-toothed smile at her, she lost her focus. And her confidence. Her board stopped feet away from him, but she kept going. She flew over it and landed in Raul's arms.

"Fancy bumping into you here," he said with a laugh.

Lei turned a dozen shades of red as the rest of her friends chuckled at Raul's joke. Any other moment, she might have enjoyed Raul's embrace, but not right now. Embarrassed, she removed herself from his lanky arms by pushing off against his chest.

"Don't get handsy!" she blurted. Her reaction was an act, and her friends knew it.

Lei wasn't sure why, but when she was alone, carving along the bike trail, tricks came easy. She was confident, daring even. She felt she could just be herself. As soon as someone was watching, especially someone she liked like Raul, she felt like she had to impress. That usually led to an epic fail.

"So, Lei, you ready to do some real skating?" Mike asked, holding up his skateboard.

Lei treasured her hand-me-down longboard. But to her friends, it was merely a mode of transportation since she didn't have a bike. *If you can't do an ollie on your board, then what's the point?* they always asked her.

They may not have appreciated her longboard, but they were always willing to share their skateboards with her and Marie, who didn't even own a board.

Lei pulled her gear from her backpack. She strapped on elbow and kneepads and then put her helmet on. It was all black with a white skull and crossbones.

Like her deck, they were hand-me-downs from her brother, and it showed. Her gear was covered in scrapes and gouges. Some of them were old, from her brother. Some glistened black from their newness. Those were the result of her falls.

The skatepark really wasn't much — at least not anymore. The city had built it ages ago, when the neighborhood wasn't so run down. She could see holes in the pavement where grind rails used to be. They had been removed because someone thought kids would get hurt on them.

All that was left now was a flatbank along one fence. The bank curled around at one end of the park to create a small half bowl with a hip. They called it the Hook because if they skated up the flatbank and around the face of bowl — and if they hit the hip just right — it'd shoot them back up to the opposite side of the bowl, which they used like a halfpipe. A pyramid with a flat top stood in the middle of it all.

None of the obstacles had copings — just roll-ins. Against the fence that separated the basketball court from the skatepark, there were a couple benches. Whoever had the rails torn out and then had a couple park benches added sure didn't know much about skateboarding. While it was a lame skatepark, it did provide them with a place that was all theirs to hang out.

As usual, Raul took the first run of the day. He started by the benches, pushing his board forward and building up enough speed to go up the flatbank. At the top, he stalled and then rock-n-rolled. He rolled down the bank and then up the pyramid. With a frontside kickturn, he headed back up the flatbank. A blunt stall at the top was followed by a frontside 180 ollie. Raul shot down the ramp and into the half bowl. He skated up its side, grabbing the nose of his board as it shot into the air in a Madonna. When he landed on his board, his tail slammed down on the deck at the top of the bowl.

Raul turned back to Lei and the rest of his crew, all smiles.

"Who can beat that?" he shouted.

For the first run of the day, Raul had stepped it up a notch, and he was getting a little showy with that Madonna. But he was the best skater among them.

At least on a skateboard, Lei secretly thought.

Next up was Javon. He started at the top of the flatbank and rolled in, shooting down the ramp straight over the pyramid. He got some air and did a 180 with an Indy grab. Then he turned around and came back at the pyramid. This

time, when he got to the top, he did an early grab, getting some air as he flew over the side of the pyramid. His landing was shady, but he pulled a few more tricks before ending his turn.

Lei watched Marie and Mike take their turns, trying ollies and kickturns. Neither was as good as Raul, or even Javon for that matter. But it was all for fun, and skating gave them an excuse to hang out.

When it was Lei's turn, Raul handed her his board while flashing her that crooked-toothed smile of his. The board was a fairly new Alien Workshop deck. Raul was also the most serious about skating, and the little cash he was able to get his hands on usually went toward gear. He didn't rely on hand-me-downs like the rest of them.

"Let's see what you can do with this," he said.

Lei took his board and pushed toward the pyramid. At the top, she did a backside kickturn so that she shot down its side and directly up the flatbank. She stepped off the deck with her front foot and popped up the board by stepping down on its tail with her back foot for a no comply. She caught its nose in her hand as she spun around in a 180 and then jumped back on the board and shot down the ramp in a move known as a bean plant. She carved around the pyramid and then pushed back toward her friends. As she skated by them, she took her back foot off the deck and then her front foot, stepping on the pavement. She flicked the board with her back foot so that it spun a 360 in the air. Then she jumped back on as its wheels hit the ground.

"What do you call that?" an older boy shouted from outside the chain-link fence.

Lei stopped and looked back. All her friends were watching as four older boys filed through the fence. They all had decks tucked under their arms and walked with cocky swaggers.

"It's a ghost-ride 360-shuvit," Lei shouted. Immediately, she began to blush.

"Never heard of that before," one of the older boys said. "Can't ya ollie?"

"A trick's a trick, and she nailed it," Raul said, taking a

step toward the older boys. That was probably the first time he had ever defended one of her longboard tricks.

Raul was the tallest member of Lei's crew, but still, the older boys were half a head taller than him.

"Who are you?" Raul asked. He was also the bravest of their bunch.

The leader of the older boys stepped up to Raul.

"I'm Gabe," he said, and looking at each of his friends, he rattled off their names. "This here's Benji, Hie, and Juan."

"And what are you doing at our skatepark?" Raul asked.

"Your skatepark?" Gabe asked. "Well, the city park we usually skate at now has No Skateboarding signs posted all over it. So we figured we head down here. It's not much, but it'll do."

"It'd be cool to have you skate with us, maybe show us some tricks," Mike said, trying to get in good with the older boys.

The older boys looked at each other and snickered. "Nah, you don't get it," Gabe said. "We're making this our park."

For emphasis, Hie stepped up to Mike and gave him a shove. Mike stumbled backward and dropped his board.

Lei saw Raul clenching his fists at his side. Even though they outnumbered the older boys five to four, none of her crew really had much experience fighting. These boys, however, had the look of a pack of wolves. She was sure they'd been in a scuffle or two.

"Come on, let's go," Lei said, grabbing one of Raul's hands. "They aren't worth it."

The look he shot her was dark and angry. She hoped that he understood why she was doing it. More importantly, she hoped he'd forgive her for dragging him away as the older boys laughed.

THE HILL

After getting kicked off their turf, Lei's friends headed home.
Except for Marie. The two girls sat down by the basketball
courts, far enough from the skatepark that their new rivals
didn't seem to care. Eventually, some of the older kids in the
neighborhood would gather to play ball. Lei and her crew
usually left before they showed. The older kids liked to harass
her friends. But they usually left her alone. They knew she
was Feng's little sister, and nobody messed with Feng.

"They aren't so hot," said Lei, watching the boys skate.

Sure, Hie hit a 360 pop shuvit, but other than some
kickflips and ollies, they weren't much better than her crew.

One of them, Juan, spent the whole time trying to nollie. Every other try or so, his skateboard would go shooting backward as he stumbled forward.

"What do you think? They're in high school, right?" Marie asked. "They look like freshmen, maybe sophomores."

"I don't know," Lei replied. "I don't remember seeing them when we started middle school last year, so probably sophomores."

"How cool would it be to hang out with them?"

"Seriously?!" Lei said. "They just kicked us off our turf."

"I know," Marie said. "But Juan's kinda cute."

"What, the guy who can't hit a nollie?"

Marie flushed. "Yeah," she said.

"If Raul heard you talking like that," Lei said, "he'd flip."

"You're the one crushing on Raul, not me," Marie teased.

With that, Lei got up. She couldn't take any more of this girl talk. What she really wanted to be doing was skating.

"You want a ride home?" she asked Marie.

"Sure," Marie said, standing up but never taking her eyes off of Juan.

"Think he'll see me if I wave goodbye?" Marie asked.

Lei set her longboard down on the pavement and pointed at it. "Just get on."

Marie stepped on with both feet over the front truck. Lei put her front foot directly behind Marie and pushed forward.

Sometimes, Lei wasn't sure why Marie even bothered coming down to the park. She didn't have her own board. She didn't skate much either, preferring to just chill in the shade and watch the boys. On the longboard, though, Marie seemed like a natural. It wasn't easy keeping up speed with both their weight on her board, but Marie kept perfect balance, so they didn't wobble at all.

When they stopped in front of her building a few blocks later, Marie asked, "So are you going to bomb the Hill?"

The Hill was the reason Lei liked going past Marie's, even if it was a bit out of her way. A couple blocks away was a steep hill that dropped down into a river valley. It met up with a road that eventually got her back to her grandparents'. Bombing the Hill was worth the climb back out of the valley to get home again.

"Yeah," Lei said with a smile.

"You're crazy," Marie said. "I rode down that hill on my

bike once. I thought I was going to go flying into the river, and that was with brakes!"

Lei just smiled as she pushed down the road.

"See you at school Monday," Marie called to her.

* * *

Once at the top of the Hill, Lei strapped on her pads and helmet. She also pulled out a pair of sliding gloves.

The Hill looked like you were dropping into a huge quarterpipe. It sloped down steeply for about a block before leveling off. Then the road went another block before a T-intersection. The road it met up with was blocked off by orange barricades, because it had been turned into a walking path along the river. When Lei got here early, like she did today, there weren't many walkers to deal with.

Just beyond the intersection was about fifty feet of grass, and after that was a railing that kept kamikaze skaters and bikers from taking a spill in the river.

Lei leaned forward and let gravity pull her down the hill. She quickly picked up speed. As she felt her board wobble a little, she crouched down. She could hear the wind whistle through her helmet straps, feel every divot in the pavement,

and see her surroundings zipping by. She felt completely free, with only her deck between her and the blur of the world.

About a block down, the street leveled out. She glanced up to see if anyone was in her path. No one.

Lei aimed for one of the gaps in the barricades. They were wide enough to let a couple bikers or walkers through at a time, but not a car.

With one gloved hand, she did an Indy grab. With the other, she reached back and dragged it along the pavement. Then she broke into a slide, shifting the weight to her front foot so she could whip the tail of her board around until it was at a 90-degree angle to the street.

Now was the tricky part. She shot through the gap. Then, as she slowed, she angled her board so that she would shoot down the walking path.

She noticed two other skaters. They were older boys with skateboards, and they were checking her out. Lei lost focus. She straightened her board out too much. Instead of zipping down the path, she headed for a curb. Her board was knocked out from under her feet, and she tumbled into the grass.

The two skater boys kicked over to her.

"You all right?" one asked.

"That was pretty wild," the other said. "You nearly made that turn."

No thanks to you guys, Lei thought.

She looked herself over. Thankfully no new road rash, since she'd tumbled into the grass. But her shoulders and knees felt a little scraped and bruised.

The boys stood there, gawking at her. She had been sitting in the grass for nearly a minute now, and neither had offered to help her up or go grab her board.

"I'm fine," Lei said finally, going to stand.

That's when they made their move, stammering and reaching for her with clumsy hands.

Too late, boys, she thought.

"I got it," she said, brushing their hands away. Then she stomped past them to go get her board.

"Is this where you usually skate?" one of them asked.

She looked back and shook her head. Then she hopped on her board and pushed away. She didn't bother to check if they were following her, but she hoped they weren't.

She was embarrassed about taking a spill right in front of them and didn't want to talk. They would probably razz her being on a longboard, just like her friends. She didn't get respect from anyone.

Sometimes, she wished she was more like her brother. Nobody messed with him. No one ever harassed him when he was out carving on his longboard.

By that night, Lei had completely forgiven Chewy. The old dog was curled up in her arms as she sat on the couch, watching TV and waiting her family to show up for dinner.

Feng burst through the door just before six. Lei didn't even need to look up to know it was him. He worked at the food-processing plant in the industrial park, and his smell announced his arrival. A mix of grease, spices, and spoiled milk wafted through the room, making her choke.

"Hey, sis," Feng said as he walked by and tousled her hair.

"Dude, go shower," Lei yelled back, trying to straighten her hair. "You reek."

She shouldn't have said that. The next thing Lei knew, her brother pinned her down and started tickling her. She sucked in big breaths of the rotten air between giggles.

"How do I smell now?" he shouted. "Get a good whiff!"

"Get off!" she shouted.

Her brother was a few years older than she was, and while he wasn't even average sized by American standards, he was bigger than she was. She was helpless.

"Feng, go shower," their mom said.

She and their father had just walked through the door. They all worked together, so the stench was just tripled.

"The sooner we get washed up, the sooner we eat," her mom added.

"Too late, the shower's mine," her dad said as he raced through the living room.

"Great," Lei pouted. "I have to sit by stinky now."

"Feng, do not sit on the couch in your work clothes," their mom scolded, saving Lei.

* * *

At dinner, Feng leaned over to whisper in her ear between mouthfuls of noodles.

"I heard you weren't at the skatepark today. Something up?"

"No, no, we were there, but only for a bit," she replied.

"I heard Gabe and his crew were using the park. They aren't causing you any trouble, are they?"

Lei knew she had to be careful here. More than once her brother had gotten into fights during high school. They led to him eventually being expelled. He never bothered going to get his GED and instead started working at the food processing plant with their folks.

She worried that if he knew the truth about what happened today, he'd start something. Some of his earlier fights nearly ended with him being thrown in juvie. If he started something now, the results could be worse.

"Nope, they were pretty cool," she lied.

OUR PARK

All that week at school, her friends talked about what had happened on Saturday. Raul was steaming about it.

"It's our park," he'd say. "They can't kick us out of our park."

"Technically, it's a public park," Marie would break in. "Anyone can skate there." She was still crushin' on Juan, though she'd only admit that to Lei.

"Then we should be able to skate there, too," Javon would add, slamming his fist down on the table and ratting his tray.

He, Raul, and Mike would eventually get so worked up that one of the teachers would come over to calm them down.

And every day, they'd vow to go back to their park next Saturday morning.

Lei knew that all of them secretly wanted to ask if her brother could help them out. Feng was respected — and a bit feared — throughout the neighborhood. At home, he was a sweet, loving brother, but she had heard stories about some of the fights he had gotten into. She didn't want that happening at the skatepark. She didn't want to feel guilty if someone got hurt, or worse.

Plus, she wanted to solve her problems on her own. It was bad enough that most of her stuff was his hand-me-downs. She didn't want to have to rely on him for everything. Lei wanted to be respected, but for being herself. Not for being Feng's little sister.

Friday night was restless for Lei. She tossed and turned as she worried about what would happen if those older boys showed up at the skatepark again. Raul might try to act all tough and pick a fight.

In the morning, her door creaked open and she heard Feng whisper, "There you go, Chewy."

Lei wasn't sure why she did what she did next. Maybe she was just sleepy. Maybe she was just tired of feeling helpless. Between her brother and those older boys, there were just too many people messing with her right now.

She leaped out of bed and started throwing things at her brother. Pillows. Shoes. Whatever she could grab.

"I knew it!" she yelled. "It's your fault he's been wrecking my skate shoes!"

Feng quickly ducked behind the door and slammed it shut, taking Chewy with him. At least she wouldn't have slimy laces today.

A moment later, the door opened again. She armed herself with a pillow as Feng poked his head through the doorway.

"Do you want me to swing by the skatepark on my break?" he asked.

"Why?" she asked.

She knew what he was hinting at. Maybe he didn't believe the lie she told last Friday, that Gabe and his friend had been cool. But this was her and her friends' problem, not his.

"I don't want you there," she said.

"Okay, just asking," Feng said. Then he shut the door.

Lei tried going back to sleep, but it was no use. She was too wound up. She got out of bed and was met with a heaping bowl of steamy rice at the kitchen table.

"Can't we mix things up a bit?" she asked. "Like pancakes. I need my carbs."

Her grandfather poked his head over his newspaper.

"Be respectful, little one," he whispered to her. And then added, more loudly, "Pancakes would be a nice change."

"Hmpf!" her grandmother huffed as she set down a glass of OJ for Lei.

Lei felt like she had just won a battle. If her grandfather was on board with mixing things up, maybe her grandma would at least consider it. Suddenly, she felt confident in herself.

After excusing herself from the table, Lei headed out the door. She cranked up some tunes and was soon carving down the street. As she hit the bike path and started cross steppin' to the dance rhythms, she realized that she had some of her own habits, kind of like her grandmamma and her congee. Maybe she needed to mix things up and stop worrying about what people thought of her longboarding.

Thanks to her restlessness and to her brother pestering her this morning, she beat all her friends to the skatepark. She geared up with her pads, and since no one was there to harass her for working on some longboard tricks, she put on her sliding gloves, too.

She pushed her board toward the flatbank, skating up it. At the top, she rolled to fakie. When she shot down the ramp, she put her weight down on her front foot and twisted her body so the tail of her board spun around 180 degrees for a powerslide.

Simple, when other people aren't harassing me, she thought.

She did a quick 180 shuvit and then pushed her board back toward the flatbank. At the top, she spun around with a frontside kickturn.

This time, as she leaned on her front foot, she spun the tail of her board all the way around for a 180 powerslide. Unlike a shuvit, her wheels stayed on the ground, screeching across the pavement as they spun around. She wobbled a little as she spun from goofy to regular, but she hit that trick and was feeling good.

Another shuvit and she was heading back up the flatbank. At the top, she did a no comply to shoot down the ramp.

Out of the corner of her eye, she saw Raul wave as he was cutting through the opening in the chain-link fence.

He's not going to trip me up today, she thought, so she went for her next trick.

As she leaned off her front foot, she did an Indy grab with one hand. She reached her other hand back and dragged it along the pavement, like she would if she were bombing down a hill. Then her back foot pushed the tail of her board so that it was doing a slide.

A slide was a way to stop on a skateboard, but it was also a way to make a quick turn, which she needed to do bombing down the Hill. So as her skateboard was about to stop, she straightened it out so that she kept rolling across the pavement. And she skated right over to Raul.

"That's a pretty slick move," Raul said.

She blushed at the compliment.

"So what's up with all those slides," Raul said, teasingly. "Can't you ollie?" He may be cute and one of the best skaters she knew, but the timing of his jokes could use some work.

"At least I'll get on a skateboard," she said. "I've never seen you try a longboard."

Then she slugged him playfully in the arm.

"Ow!" he said, grabbing her hands. "Why'd I deserve that?"

As they stood there, Raul smiled down at her. All she could think about was how white his teeth were. How warm his hands were in hers.

"Are you two gonna kiss?" Marie shouted as she hopped over the fence.

Lei turned away, blushing.

"Don't be silly," Raul said. "Kiss Lei? No way."

She was about to punch him in the arm again, less playfully this time, but she heard someone carving down the street. They all looked, expecting to see Javon and Mike. It was the high schoolers from last week. Gabe and his friends were headed their way.

She glanced at her friends. Raul had a look of anger mixed with concern. He was probably worried that Javon and Mike weren't around — it was just him and two girls to face Gabe's crew. Even worse, judging by the way Marie was eyeing Juan, it seemed that only Lei was in his corner.

"Hey, look, it's the newbs," Gabe shouted as he and his crew skated through the opening in the chain link fence.

"This is our park now," Hie said.

The way they strutted, with heads tilted forward and hands clenched, Lei knew they meant business. Raul met them halfway, with the same serious stance. Lei and Marie

47

scrambled to follow him, with Marie making sure that she ended up across from Juan.

"We were here first," Raul shot back.

"I don't care," Gabe said, getting in Raul's face. "It's our park now."

Lei could feel the tension growing toward a fight if Raul didn't back down. Between the breaks in Raul and Gabe's shouting, she heard the familiar sound of composite wheels carving along pavement. She looked up, worried that it was the rest of her crew, Mike and Javon. If they showed, things would definitely escalate.

Instead, it was the two boys she had seen last weekend. The two that had watched her bomb down the Hill and lose it.

"So this is where you skate?" one of them shouted to her as he cut through the opening in the fence.

"We've spent all morning trying to find where you hang out to skate," the other said.

Everyone turned toward the two new kids entering the park. "What are you guys doing here?" Gabe scowled.

"Looking for a new place to skate," one of the boys

replied. "Same as you, since we can't do it at the city park anymore."

"I didn't even know this place existed," the other boy replied.

Lei didn't know if this made matters worse or not. The boys knew Gabe and his buds, which could be bad for her and her crew if they were all friends. Yet Gabe seemed to be backing away a little as the new boys joined things.

One of them walked right up to Lei.

"Hey, I'm Bobby," he said. "The way you were bombing down the Hill on your longboard, I didn't know if we'd find you at a skatepark."

"This is just where me and my friends like to hang out," she replied, trying to sound cool and confident with the older boy's attention focused on her.

"Cool if we join you?" he asked.

Now things were getting even weirder for Lei. She had some older boy talking to her like they were buds. Out of the corner of her eye she could see Marie grinning, thinking Lei was scoring with a high schooler. Meanwhile, Raul had a hint of concern furrowing his brow.

She needed to get a handle on the situation before something bad happened.

"Sure," Lei replied. "You can skate with us."

The vibe of these new boys was so different from that of Gabe and his friends. They sauntered more than strutted. While they had an air of confidence about them, they also seemed pretty at ease, relaxed, and friendly. She hoped they'd like her crew. "This is Marie and Raul," she said.

When she said Raul's name, she reached out and touched his arm. Hopefully, he would get it. She was letting him know that these guys were cool.

"Wait a second," Gabe said. "There ain't room enough here for all of us."

The tone of Gabe's voice raised the tensions again. Lei could see it in the way her friends backed away.

"Yeah, this place isn't much," Bobby said. "Not compared to the park, so let's skate for it."

"What?" Raul asked.

"Okay," Gabe said. "My crew against them three."

"Nah, I'll skate with them," Bobby said. "That one girl doesn't even have a board."

Bobby pointed to Marie, and she went from looking afraid to being relieved.

Gabe seemed a little unsure about things, but eyeing up Raul and Lei, a smirk crossed his face.

"Sure."

"So here are the rules," Bobby began. "We'll pair off, skating *mano a mano*. Each person takes a run, say two to three minutes, to wow us with some tricks. Then the judges will decide who wins. We have three pairs, so it'll be a best of three competition."

They drew names, and it was decided that Benji would be paired against Bobby, Juan against Raul, and Lei would have to skate against Gabe.

Marie and Hie and the other new boy, whose name was Luke, would judge. Winning team would get the skatepark on Saturday mornings while the losers would have to find another time.

Things started off well for Lei's crew. Bobby skated first, and she quickly learned why he had that air of confidence about him. He was good.

He rolled in and shot down the flatbank and then up the pyramid, where he ollied up and kickflipped his board. He landed on the other side of the pyramid. After getting to the flat part of the skate park, he did a 360 pop shuvit, spinning his board completely around in the air under his feet. Next, he headed for the halfpipe. He shot up one side, catching the lip with his front wheels, then rolled to fakie, shooting up the other side. He caught the lip between his back wheels and tail for a blunt slide, and then did an ollie pop, his wheels slapping down on the concrete with a loud *TUNK*!

His ride was smooth, and he hit nearly every trick, which was more than she could say for Benji. He tried grinding across one of the benches and fell off his board. And in general, he just didn't push things as hard as Bobby. But when the votes were tallied, Marie and Luke voted for Bobby, Hie for Benji.

Bobby looked over at Hie and shook his head. "So that's how it's gonna be, huh?" he said.

Hie just shrugged his shoulders.

Next up was Juan. He was more solid than Benji. He ollied up to a boardslide across the edge of one of the benches. As he skated up the pyramid, he attempted a nollie with a heelflip at the top. But he missed it, falling hard on the cement with his board scooting out from under him. The rest of his run was a few flips and ollies, but nothing outstanding.

Then it was Raul's turn, and he started angry. He ollied up to do a nose grind across the same bench that Juan did his trick on. Lei could tell that was trying to one up his competition. Then he skated up the pyramid, and instead of going for a nollie heelflip at the top, as Lei suspected, he went for a nollie 180, and just missed landing. But he was able to quickly jump back on his board. For his last trick, he shifted his weight back on his board's tail and circled around the pyramid while doing a manual. Then hit a quick kickflip to end his run.

When it came time to vote, Lei saw Juan wink at Marie, and that was it. Her vote was his. Hie also voted for Juan while Luke voted for Raul.

Raul cast Marie a dark look, but Marie didn't even notice.

Lei thought Raul's run was more solid, but like Marie, she might have been pulling for the boy that she was crushin' on.

With the score 1 to 1, Gabe was up. He started by dropping into the halfpipe. He skated up one side for a frontside kickturn and then went up the other side, caught the lip with his front wheels and then rocked to fakie. There was just enough vert on the halfpipe for Gabe to get some air, and he even hit a 180 frontside ollie with an Indy grab. After that, he shot out of the halfpipe to the flat area of the park and did a manual around the pyramid, ending with a kickflip, just like Raul.

Gabe was all smiles as he walked by a grimacing Raul.

"We got this," he said to Benji and Juan, giving them high fives.

His run was definitely solid, probably second only to Bobby's. Lei was feeling nervous, like she was going to let her friends down.

Raul walked up to her and held out his board.

"You can do this, Lei," he said.

She wasn't so sure. Street tricks weren't her thing. Sure, she could ollie and kickflip and manual. But not like Raul.

Not like Gabe. The street course was their turf. Her course was actually the street. Then she got an idea. A daring one.

"I don't need that," she said to Raul.

Raul looked confused.

"What?" he asked.

"Just don't say anything," she said.

"Huh?"

That seemed to confuse him even more, so she leaned in close and whispered, "Whenever people mess with me about my longboard, I get nervous, like it's not good enough to be myself. Especially when it's you."

"I never meant —" Raul stammered. His blush told her that he got her meaning.

Lei geared up with her helmet and pads and sliding gloves.

"What are those for?" Gabe asked, pointing at her gloves. "Plan on falling a lot?"

Lei grabbed her longboard and jumped on.

"Follow me if you can keep up," she yelled back at everyone.

THE REAL STREET COURSE

Everyone followed Lei. She knew she didn't have much time, so she pushed as hard as she could. And she didn't bother doing any tricks on the way. No one would be as impressed by them as they would by what she was about to do: bomb the Hill.

Everyone was about a half a block behind her when she reached the top of the Hill. She only paused for a moment, just to sigh out a deep breath, before dropping into the river valley.

She crouched down as she sped up, and the board began to wobble. Then the street leveled off, and she prepared for her slide. When she pushed the tail around to start the slide this time, she didn't do an Indy grab. Instead, she reached back with both hands. She felt their plastic pucks in the palms of her hands scraping across the pavement.

Lei shot through a gap in the barricades with the wheels of her skateboard screeching across the pavement. Once past the barricades, she was going slow enough that she was able to let her forward momentum lift her up so that her hands were no longer scraping the pavement. Staying crouched down, she angled her board slightly so that she started moving parallel to the approaching curb and shot down the walking path.

She nailed it!

Standing up, she raised her hands in victory and heard the distant hoots of her friends from the top of the Hill.

* * *

Gabe's jaw dropped as he saw Lei break from her powerslide and shoot out of sight down the walking path.

"My vote's for her," Marie said.

"Mine, too," Luke added.

Gabe whipped around and glared at them.

"How can that count?" he asked. "We weren't even at the skatepark."

"The goal was to wow us," Raul said. "And you gotta be impressed by that trick."

Gabe looked to his crew for support, but they were still eyeing up the Hill.

"That girl is nuts," Benji said.

"Yeah, man," Hie added. "I wouldn't try that on my board."

"So is your vote for her, too?" Gabe asked.

"Doesn't matter, dude," Hie said. "But if you could do what she just did, you'd get my vote."

Gabe looked down on the Hill. He seemed to shrink as doubt sunk in.

"Whatever," he said, shaking his head.

Gabe skated off with his crew following him. All except for Juan. He skated over to Marie.

"So what grade are you in?" he asked.

"Eighth," she replied. "You?"

"Ninth," he said. "I just moved here, and Gabe was the first skater I met, so I hooked up with his crew."

They were all smiles as they chatted.

* * *

Lei beat everyone back to the skatepark, even though she had to hike back up out of the valley. She was happy to see that Raul was leading the pack, followed by Bobby and Luke. That meant her trick had wowed everyone. Heck, she had wowed herself. She could still feel the adrenaline pumping through her veins. When she got home, she'd be sure to tell her brother about what happened today. Well, about her bombing the Hill, not about Gabe and his friends.

"Where's Marie?" Lei asked Raul.

"Oh, I think she's made a new friend," Raul said with a smile as he skated up to her.

With his crooked smile, he let Lei know that he was cool with Marie, even though she had voted against him.

As they talked, Bobby and Luke started skating up and down the flatbank to work on some tricks.

Raul leaned down and picked up Lei's longboard. He twirled it around in his hand and then flicked one of the wheels so that it spun and spun.

"I still think that it's weird you skate on this," he said.

"There's no kicktail. I'm surprised you can do any tricks at all."

She wasn't sure what to make of that, to feel hurt or shoot back some smart-alecky response.

Then he asked, "Think you could teach me how to slide like that?"

"Sure," she said with a smile.

Now that Lei has taught Raul some longboard skills, they get together and skate a few times a week. They pretend it's just to bomb the Hill, but they always end up going to get something to eat afterward.

Her story has inspired custom skateboard and sticker designs.

L2S Daring

L2S Tían Hawk Face

L2S Chewy!

SKATE CLINIC:
360 OLLIE

1. While rolling, shift your feet into position. Your front foot should be right behind or over the front trucks. Place the ball of your back foot on the edge of the board, right at the base of the tail.

2. Bend your knees and turn your shoulders and arms in the opposite direction of your planned spin. You are preparing to ollie.

3. Ollie hard and turn, scooping your board with your back foot so that it spins 360 degrees along with your body.

4. As you land, bend your knees to absorb the impact. Try to land with all four wheels hitting the ground together to maintain control on your skateboard.

SKATE CLINIC:
TERMS

bean plant
a move where the skater grabs the nose of the board while stepping off and planting his or her front foot on the ground or ramp, with the back foot still on the board, then jumps back on the board and rolls away

heelflip
a move where the skater flips the board over with his or her heel

Indy grab
a grab where the skater places his or her back hand on the toeside of the board

kickflip
a move where the rider pops the skateboard into the air and flicks it with the front foot to make it flip all the way around in the air before landing on the board again

no comply
a move where the skater does an ollie movement using only the back foot while the front foot is planted on the ground

nollie
a move where the skater snaps the nose of the skateboard to pop the entire board into the air with his or her feet

nosegrind
a move where the skater grinds across the obstacle with only the front truck

ollie
a move where the rider pops the skateboard into the air with his or her feet

pop shuvit
a move where the skater ollies and spins the board 180 degrees before landing on the board again

shuvit
a move where the skater jumps and spins the board 180 degrees underneath him or her before landing on the board

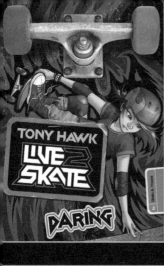

TONY HAWK
LIVE2 SKATE
DARING
by Blake A. Hoena

TONY HAWK
LIVE2 SKATE
Fresh
by Michael A. Steele

TONY HAWK
LIVE2 SKATE
FEARLESS
by Shawnee Tease

TONY HAWK
LIVE2 SKATE
STRONG
by Matthew K. Manning

HOW DO YOU LIVE?

written by
BLAKE A. HOENA

Blake A. Hoena grew up in central Wisconsin, where he wrote stories about robots conquering the moon and trolls lumbering around the woods behind his parents' house. He now lives in Minnesota and continues to write about fun things like space aliens and superheroes. Blake has written more than fifty chapter books and graphic novels for children.

pencils and colors by
FERNANDO CANO

Fernando Cano is an all-around artist living in Monterrey, Mexico. He currently works as a concept artist for video game company CGbot. Having published with Marvel, DC, Pathfinder, and IDW, he spends his free time playing video games, singing, writing, and above all, drawing!

inks by
LAURA RIVERA

Laura Rivera lives in San Nicolas, Mexico. She currently works as a concept artist in the video game industry, doing what she loves most: drawing! During her free time, she enjoys building projects, photography, and playing with her dog.